Barbie™
PINK-TASTIC!

Illustrated by Pamela Duarte
and Chris Musselman

A GOLDEN BOOK • NEW YORK

BARBIE and associated trademarks and trade dress are owned by, and used under license from, Mattel.
Copyright © 2016 Mattel. All Rights Reserved.
www.barbie.com
Published in the United States by Golden Books, an imprint of Random House Children's Books, a division of
Penguin Random House LLC, 1745 Broadway, New York, NY 10019, and in Canada by Random House of Canada,
a division of Penguin Random House Ltd., Toronto. Golden Books, A Golden Book, and the G colophon are
registered trademarks of Penguin Random House LLC.
ISBN 978-1-101-93248-3
randomhousekids.com
Printed in the United States of America
10 9 8 7 6 5 4 3 2

Hi, I'm Barbie! I love pink!

How many times can you find the word
PINK in the puzzle below?

```
P   I   N   P   K   I   N   K   P   I
I   P   I   N   K   P   I   N   P   N
K   N   I   P   I   N   I   K   I   P
N   P   I   K   N   I   P   K   N   I
I   K   N   P   I   P   N   I   K   K
P   N   I   P   I   N   K   N   I   P
```

ANSWER: 8.

Barbie and Lacey are ready to go, go, go!

Barbie and her friends are going to the fair.

STATE FAIR

Barbie and Nikki stop for a sweet treat.

Barbie and Teresa are tickled pink
at the fun house.

Barbie and her friends make a splash.

Lacey and Barbie dive in!

Super slide!

Fun in the sun.

Barbie and Nikki go fishing.

So fluffy!

Can you find the teddy bear that is different?

A

B

C

D

E

Off to the petting zoo!

Fuzzy friends.

Barbie and Nikki have fun feeding the cute calves.

Cute and cuddly.

"This little lamb is friendly," says Teresa.

Barbie loves horses.

Barbie is going to ride in the horse show.

Barbie and Tawny make a great team.

Barbie and Teresa brush their horses.

Can you find the 5 differences between the top and bottom pictures?

Nikki pets a pretty pony.

Nikki and Teresa have a spooky time.

Barbie is a judge at the flower show.

Snack time!

Look up, down, foward, and backward to find these fun words from the fair.

rides · candy · popcorn · toys
games · animals

```
R A Z T U V B C D F
I Y D N A C E J K L
D W N M A R I U S O
E D P G H U V X F R
S Y O T W C A L I N
T W P Y I H L Z G Q
Q A C K Y G A M E S
E N O D I N E P O T
V J R M E L A N I E
Z A N I M A L S C H
```

Teresa enters a baking contest.

Yummy!

Barbie practices a new song.

Teresa is terrific on the keyboard.

Nikki plays it loud.

Connect the dots to see Barbie's favorite instrument.

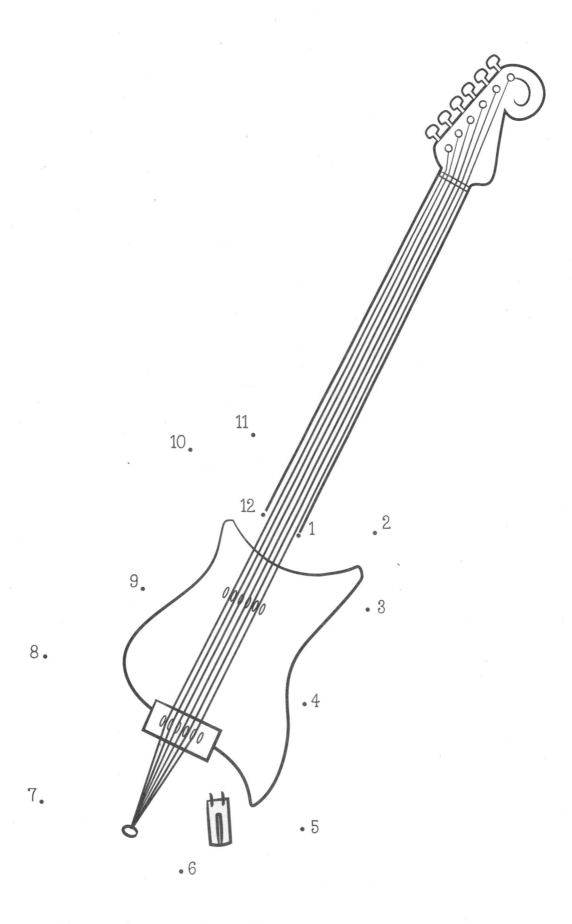

Barbie rocks out.

Barbie, Teresa, and Nikki dance to the beat.

Nikki and Teresa love the
costumes Barbie created.

Barbie and her friends are ready to rock.

Best friends rock!

Barbie, Teresa, and Nikki win the talent show!

Super stars.

Up, up, and away!

Smile!

Draw a picture of yourself and your friends.

Barbie™

Pink Party!

Barbie and Skipper are ready
for sand and sunshine.

Swim buddies.

Sunshiny day!

Pool party!

Barbie is a good chef.

Look up, down, backward, and
foward for Barbie's favorite foods.

hamburger · hotdogs · salad
smoothies · fruit · tacos

```
C H A M B U R G E R
S M O O T H I E S A
F G T H I K L D T N
A N D A L A S K I O
B E O R M U D E U Z
G F G L I L L I R B
T P S O C A T N F Z
Q I H Y C H X Y I K
O J H O T D O G S L
```

Barbie loves being a big sister.

Sister hug!

Can you find the 5 differences between the top and bottom pictures?

ANSWER: In the bottom picture, the backpack is missing her sunglasses, the "B" on her shirt, the pocket on her pants, and her shoelace loop.

Chelsea loves to dance in her
pretty pink dress!

Barbie is on her toes, too!

Connect the dots to see Barbie's surprise for Chelsea.

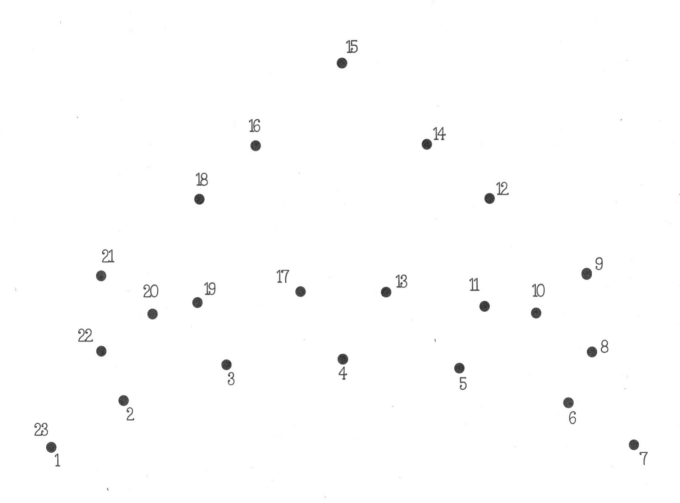

Chelsea loves animals.

Best furry friends.

so cute!

Barbie™

Stacie loves soccer.

Barbie gets ready to practice with Stacie.

Smile!

Slam dunk, Stacie!

Skipper loves to listen to music.

Barbie creates a new song.

Skipper is creative and connected.

Twist and twirl.

Red-carpet photo.

Pretty as a princess.

Super sporty.

Sweet and stylish.

Glam and glitzy.

Cool and casual.

Lunchtime!

Pet party!

Pup-tastic pets!

Chow time!

Lacey makes it messy!

Purr-fect!

Adorable *fur*-ever!

Baking with sisters is the best!

Sister fun!

Delicious treats.

Connect the dots to see a sweet surprise.

Skipper creates a special design.

Yummy cakes!

Super supper!

Dinner or dessert?

Dance party!

Nice moves!

Stacie plays the tambourine.

Skipper's got the beat!

Chelsea sings out loud.

Sister jam!

Sister selfie!

Use the code below to show Barbie's message to her sisters.

S =   I =   T =   E =

R =   A =   H =   B =

Bedtime!

Brush! Brush! Brush!

Sweet dreams!

Chelsea hears a thunderstorm.

Knock, knock! Who's awake?

Chelsea wakes up Stacie.

Chelsea wakes up Skipper.

The sisters go to Barbie's room.

Skipper and Chelsea wake up Barbie.

Time for a slumber party!

Create a sensational slumber-party door hanger!

- Decorate your door hanger.

- Ask an adult to help you cut out the door hanger.

- Place the door hanger on your doorknob.

High five!

Chelsea braids Barbie's hair.

Chelsea makes beautiful flower necklaces!
Here is one for you!

- Color the flowers.
- Ask an adult to help you cut out the flowers and punch a hole where indicated.
- Wtih an adult's help, cut a piece of yarn about 16 inches long.
- Thread the yarn through the hole in each flower.
- Ask an adult to tie the two ends of the yarn loosely around your neck.

Sleepover snacks!

Terrific treats!

Chelsea can't wait to watch a movie.

Game time!

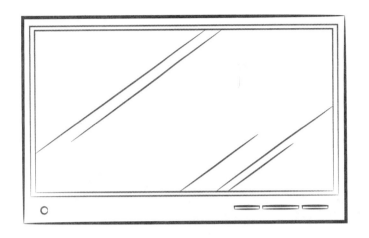

Good-night hug!

Barbie, Skipper, Stacie, and Chelsea are
going to the amusement park for
Chelsea's birthday.

Stacie and Chelsea paddle along the lake.

Barbie bumps into her sisters.

Time to bounce!

Chelsea and Stacie go for a ride.

Chelsea loves her beautiful pink balloon.

Chelsea pretends to be a fairy.

Barbie wins a prize!

Chelsea loves her pink-tastic party!